Little Rabbit's Christmas

HARRY HORSE

Ω

PEACHTREE
ATLANTA

In memory of
Harry and Mandy,
Roo, Chiquita, and Steve.

Published by
PEACHTREE PUBLISHERS
1700 Chattahoochee Avenue
Atlanta, Georgia 30318-2112
www.peachtree-online.com

Illustrations created in pen and ink and watercolor.
First published in Great Britain in 2007 by Penguin Books.

Printed in China
10 9 8 7 6 5 4 3 2 1
First Edition

Library of Congress Cataloging-in-Publication Data

Horse, Harry.
Little Rabbit's Christmas / written and illustrated by Harry Horse. -- 1st ed.
p. cm.
Summary: When the Christmas Rabbit makes his wish come true and brings him the beautiful red sled from the store window, Little Rabbit wants it all to himself until he learns that even the best gift is better when shared.
ISBN 13: 978-1-56145-419-8
ISBN 10: 1-56145-419-2
[1. Sleds--Fiction. 2. Selfishness--Fiction. 3. Christmas--Fiction. 4. Rabbits--Fiction.] I. Title.
PZ7.H7885Lmc 2007
[E]--dc22
2006103194

One Christmas Eve, when the snow lay all around,
Little Rabbit saw something that he really liked.
"Look, Papa! A beautiful sled!"
Papa agreed that it was a lovely sled.

When they got home, Little Rabbit told his mama all about the sled. "It is red," said Little Rabbit. "And it goes *Whoosh!*"

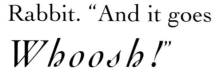

Mama asked Little Rabbit to help his brothers and sisters decorate the Christmas tree. But Little Rabbit did not want to . . .

Instead he watched the snow falling outside the burrow.

"I wish I had a sled," he sighed.

That night, Mama tucked Little Rabbit into bed and read him a story.

She told Little Rabbit that if he was good, the Christmas Rabbit would leave some lovely presents in the stocking at the end of his bed.

"Will he bring me a sled?" wondered Little Rabbit.
He did not think that the red sled could fit in such
a little stocking.

"Go to sleep, Little Rabbit," said Mama. "Who
knows what the Christmas Rabbit will bring?"

The next morning, his brothers and sisters got up early.
"Wake up, Little Rabbit," they cried. "It's Christmas morning!"

Little Rabbit was very excited.

He looked in his stocking.

He found a bouncy blue ball,
a yo-yo, and a pair of mittens . . .

but no sled.

"Where's my sled?" asked Little Rabbit.

Little Rabbit looked under the
Christmas tree to see if the sled was there.
Then he looked up the chimney
to see if it had gotten stuck.

He even looked under Mama and Papa's bed.
"It's not fair!" cried Little Rabbit. "I only wanted a sled."

"Dry your eyes, Little Rabbit, and look outside," said Papa.

It was the red sled! Little Rabbit was so happy.
"The Christmas Rabbit came," he told everyone.
"And he brought me a sled!"

Papa tied a rope on the sled so that Little Rabbit could
pull it across the snow.
"Put your mittens on," said Mama. "It's cold outside."
"Mittens are for babies, Mama," said Little Rabbit.
And off he ran into the snow, pulling the red sled behind him.

Everybody loved the red sled.
"It's mine," said Little Rabbit. "The
Christmas Rabbit brought it to me."

Little Rabbit was so excited about his new sled that he didn't want to share it. "It's not fair," said Little Rabbit. "Everybody wants to play with my sled!"

So Little Rabbit took the sled far away
to a place where he could play with it by himself.

Little Rabbit pulled the sled up a hill.

Whoosh!

Down the hill he flew.

"Look at me!" he cried.
But nobody was looking.

"I'll show them how fast I can go," said
Little Rabbit.
So he climbed the biggest hill he could find.

Whoosh! down the hill he flew on the red sled,
faster and faster.

"Look out!" cried Little Rabbit. The sled was going too fast.
He flew through a hedge, over a frozen stream, and then . . .

...*Crash!*

Little Rabbit flew off
and landed in the snow.

The red sled was broken.

Little Rabbit climbed back up the hill, dragging
the broken sled behind him.

It was such a long way back up to the top. His nose got cold.
His little paws got colder. He wished that he had worn his new mittens.

The snow got deeper.

Little Rabbit got stuck in a snowdrift.

"Help!" cried Little Rabbit. "I'm stuck!"

Molly Mouse came running.
"Don't worry," she said.
"I'll help you. Hold on."
Molly Mouse put on her new
snowshoes and pulled Little Rabbit
out of the snow.

Benjamin and Rachel came along. They looked at the red sled.
"It's broken," said Little Rabbit.

"I can fix it with my new tools," said Benjamin.
"I can paint it with my new brushes," said Rachel.
Little Rabbit was so happy.

When the sled was mended, Little Rabbit's
friends helped him pull it back up the hill.

When they got to the top, they all climbed on to the sled.
"Hold on!" said Molly Mouse, and off they flew
down the hill.

"Look at us!" cried Little Rabbit. It was the best fun he had ever had.

"Again!" cried Little Rabbit.

They played with the sled all day.

When the sun was setting over the snowy field, Little Rabbit
invited his friends home for a Christmas party.

Little Rabbit helped Papa light the Christmas candles, and they danced around the tree and sang carols.

They played games and ate delicious food.

After Little Rabbit's friends left,
Papa carried him to bed.

"*Whoosh* . . ." said Little Rabbit sleepily. "Christmas is
good, Papa, but sharing it with friends is even better."

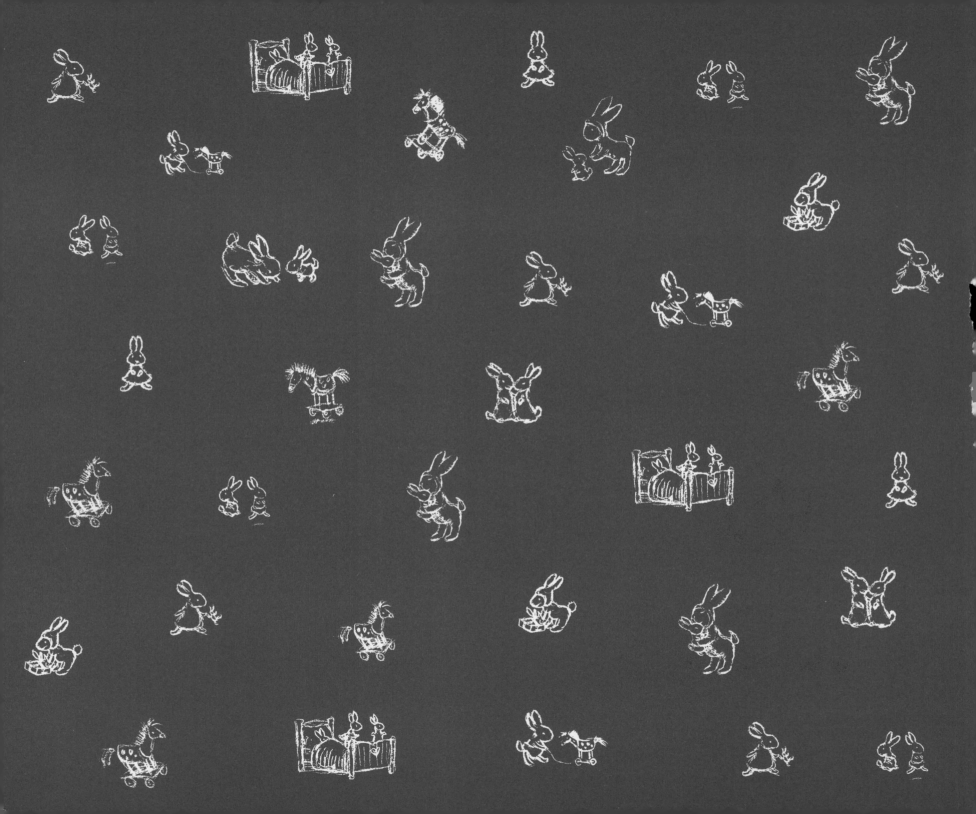